The Glitter Wand and a Frog Named Aady Lou

Written By: Sally Baldwin & Kristin Maggio

Illustrated By: Kristin Maggio

WWW.KRISTINSARTAVENUE.COM

ISBN:
PUBLISHED BY: KRISTIN'S ART AVENUE
 2ND EDITION

This book is dedicated to Jhen – Forever sending glitter your way.

A special thank you to Papa for always believing in me. We love you very much.

Also sending a special thanks to Sally- the most magical person we know.

"A little glitter your way to shine some light
To help you find your strength to make it through your plight
Though the road ahead can seem dark and weary
A little glimmer of hope will guide you merely
To all of those you love and hold dear
With just a little glitter there is nothing to fear"

As she swam across the pond she was born in, Aady Lou felt at home. She lived on the sunny side of the pond where water lilies grew and cat tails stood tall. There were many frog things to eat, and she had many frog friends around her. It was understood by all frogs that the sunny side of the pond was safe, and the dark side was not. She had heard many stories over the years about the dark side of the pond. There were stories of a place filled with snapping turtles, snakes, and many other things not good for a frog. Aady Lou even heard stories about a strange and magical land. She never ventured past the third willow tree on the ponds edge, but she always remained curious.

One day the clouds darkened in the sky and a sudden rain fell onto the pond. Aady Lou was resting on her favorite lily pad and was taken by surprise as the rain drops began to pound the water around her. She jumped into the pond and began to swim towards the shore. The rain made the water cloudy, and she couldn't tell where she was going. Frantically, she reached the edge and jumped onto the bank. She looked up and saw many trees that led into a dark forest. Aady Lou realized she was on the wrong side of the pond. She heard a loud splashing sound behind her and was worried she was in danger. She hopped very quickly, straight into the forest and was afraid to look back.

Over fallen logs and deep moss Aady Lou jumped and jumped. It seemed to grow quiet, and the rain had stopped. Nothing looked familiar to her. She heard a sigh and looked high up in a tree. Aady Lou saw an owl sitting on a branch with his head held low. She couldn't help but notice how sad he looked. Afraid to be seen, she hopped away as quietly as she could.

After hopping over many logs, Aady Lou decided to stop and rest. Just then, she noticed something shiny wedged between two rocks. Much to her surprise, she pulled out a shiny wand. Aady Lou thought it was the most beautiful thing she had ever seen. She was so taken by the wand's beauty that she didn't realize she wasn't feeling afraid anymore. Determined to find her way home, she continued to make her way through the forest.

Suddenly, there was a scurrying sound, and Aady Lou saw a mouse. She politely asked the mouse if it could point her in the direction of her pond. The mouse did not answer, but scurried back under a tree root. Aady Lou stood and watched as it came out squeaking frantically.

"My children are gone! Where are my children, oh, dear!" squeaked the mother mouse. She darted back under the tree root and then popped back out again, shouting to Aady Lou, "Help me, my children are gone!"

"Well, perhaps you should start looking where you saw them last," Aady Lou said calmly.

"Last? Well, our nest is under the tree root, and they are not there. I was only gone a minute to gather seed, and now they are gone-all five of them. Oh dear, you must help me please!" the mouse pleaded to Aady Lou.

Always known for being a good jumper, Aady Lou decided she would jump as high as she could to see if she could spot the baby mice somewhere. She jumped up and didn't see anything. She jumped again and still did not spot the mice.

On her third jump, when Aady Lou was high in the air, glitter came out of the wand she was holding and sprinkled all around. Aady Lou stared at the wand with surprise. After a moment, she heard several small voices saying, "Wow, did you see that? It's so pretty! Do it again, do it again! "

As the mother mouse watched the glitter, she remembered moving her babies high up in a tree hole, to protect them from the rain. Aady Lou saw five little mice smiling down at her. With a leap of joy, the mother mouse said "Oh, thank you, my children are safe. I am sorry, but I do not know the way back to your pond. My name is Fran, and you are welcome to stay with us." Aady Lou thanked Fran, but she needed to find her way home.

Not long before many hops and leaps, Aady Lou came upon a turtle. The turtle was flipped over on his shell with four feet in the air, running to nowhere.

"Help, help, I am up and should be down-please help me!" said the turtle.

Aady Lou just stood blinking at the sight of an upside down turtle. "How can I help?"

"Can you make my feet touch the ground instead of the air?" said the turtle. "Please turn me over".

Aady Lou tried to turn the turtle over. He was heavier than she thought. She tried again, but the turtle just rocked back and forth on his shell. She had to take a moment to think about how she could help this poor turtle out.

Then, she had an idea. She backed up and hopped to the turtle as fast as she could. With all of her might, she was going to flip the turtle over! Just as she reached him, glitter fell from the wand, and sprinkled all around. At last, the turtle felt his feet touch the ground. Aady Lou was amazed by the wand. This was the second time it helped her today.

"Ah, thank you. My name is Bart. What brings a frog to the forest?" the turtle asked.

"I am lost," said Aady Lou with a sigh. "Do you know how I can get to the sunny side of the pond?"

"I am sorry, but I do not know the way," the turtle replied. He waved goodbye as he slowly made his way to the underbrush.

The wand made Aady Lou feel safe as she made her way through the forest. When she came to a small clearing, a ray of sunshine came through the clouds. As she warmed herself on a rock, Aady Lou noticed a small berry bush beside her. There was a spider web in one of the branches, and it seemed to be moving.

It was moving from the struggle of a beautiful blue butterfly.

"Um, excuse me, Miss Frog. Can you please help me out of this sticky web? The owner of the web will be returning soon for dinner. I'd rather not be here when he gets back. Do you think you could, perhaps, unstick me?" asked the butterfly.

Aady Lou knew she must help, and hopped over to examine the web. She stood as tall as a frog could, raised the wand to the web, and tried to knock the butterfly loose. The web was sticking to the wand, so Aady Lou began waving it back and forth. Glitter slowly began to fall from the wand and sprinkled all over the butterfly. The butterfly's wings were quickly fluttering, and she was able to take flight. Aady Lou couldn't believe it. This was the third time the wand had helped today. Happy to be free, the butterfly turned to Aady Lou and thanked her. Aady Lou was happy to see the butterfly free, but was sad to be alone again. Holding the wand tight, she continued her journey home.

As Aady Lou was moving through the forest, a shadow passed over her with a flutter. Suddenly, a crow stood before her.

"Well, I see you are new around here. Lost your way, have you?" said the crow.

"Yes, I am looking for the sunny side of the pond, but I can't seem to find it," Aady Lou replied.

"Oh," the crow said with delight, "I have never met anyone from the sunny side of the pond. You are almost there. If you look through those trees, you will see the sun making the water sparkle. That's your home."

"It is?" said Aady Lou. She jumped with joy! As she jumped, glitter fell from the wand and caught the crow's attention.

"Wow, you found the glitter wand! The owl has been missing it for a long time," said the crow.

Aady Lou remembered seeing the owl, and she thought about how sad he looked. "Well, this is a magical wand, so I can understand why the owl would be missing it. "

"Magic, what makes you think the wand has magic?" said the crow.

"Because it helped a mouse find her babies when they were lost. It helped a turtle turn over after he was upside down in his shell. It even saved a butterfly from being stuck in a web. I don't know about you, but I'd say that's very special magic!" said Aady Lou.

The crow blinked, and after a moment said, "I saw all of those things while I was flying, and the wand didn't do any of them. You helped the mouse find her babies by jumping high and spotting them. You helped the turtle by turning him over in his shell. Your determination helped the butterfly out of the web. That wasn't the wand at all-that was you. "

"Really?" Aady Lou said with surprise. "But if the wand isn't magical, why is the owl looking for it?"

"I have no idea," said the crow. "But I don't think it has anything to do with magic".

Aady Lou looked through the trees towards her home. The thought of seeing her friends, and her favorite lily pad made her smile. Just as she was about to jump, she thought of the owl in the tree.

She looked at the wand and knew what she had to do. She turned around and began jumping in opposite direction.

"Hey, where are you going?" called the crow.

"I am returning the wand to the owl!" Aady Lou said happily.

Once again, Aady Lou was lost. She came to a quiet part of the forest and sat wondering what to do. Just then, she heard a sigh. She looked up and saw the owl sitting in a tree. Very slowly, she approached him.

In a quiet voice she said, "Hello, Mr. Owl, I think I found something that belongs to you."

He looked at her with wide eyes. She gazed up at him, unsure what would happen.

Just as she was beginning to think this was a bad idea, she saw the smallest tear trickle down his cheek. A smile came to his face as he looked at her. She was no longer afraid of the owl. He reached down and picked her up.

"Thank you for finding this for me. I haven't seen it in such a long time." The owl smiled and said, "This is very special to me."

"Is it special because it's a magical wand?" asked Aady Lou. She was eager for the answer.

The owl looked at her with surprise, "Not that I know of."

"If it doesn't have magic, then why is it so special?" asked Aady Lou.

"This once belonged to someone very dear to me. That's what makes it special," the owl explained.

"I am glad you have it back," said Aady Lou. "But, I wish it was magical so it could help me find my way home. I need to get to the sunny side of the pond."

The owl flew to the ground and sat Aady Lou down, gently. "I will guide you home," he said.

"You will?" Aady Lou said and jumped joyfully.

"Yes, and remember, you will always have a friend here in the forest," said the owl.

Then, the owl spread his wings as he flew in the sky. Aady Lou saw the owl hold the wand up high as he soared. She stared at the beautiful sight happening before her eyes. There was a rainbow of glitter in the sky, and it was slowly falling to the ground and forming a path in front of her. She realized the path from the glitter wand would guide her home.

As she followed the path of glitter through the forest, she came across the turtle who thanked her again for turning him over. Then, she passed the mice who all stopped scurrying to wave goodbye to her. Finally, she could see her pond through the trees. The water was sparkling from the sunlight. Aady Lou was finally home.

She found her favorite lily pad and felt happy as she sat on top of it. The owl watched to make sure she arrived home safely. She smiled as she saw the owl make his way back to the forest.

Some of Aady Lou's frog friends swam over to her when they saw her. They missed Aady Lou and wondered what had happened to her, and where she'd been. She told them of all of her adventures with the glitter wand in the forest. Not one of her frog friends believed her. Just then, the most peculiar thing happened. Glitter began falling all around them in the pond. Looking up, they saw the glitter falling from the wings of a beautiful blue butterfly. Aady Lou smiled warmly at her new friend and watched as the butterfly flew away. From that day, Aady Lou was known as the bravest frog in the pond.

As the years went on, Aady Lou would often wonder about the wand and if it was really magical. She could never be certain, but there was one thing she was sure of-something she had learned from her time in the forest. Believing in yourself and helping others makes you feel magical within.